Dear Parents:

Congratulations! Your child is taking the first steps on an exciting journey. The destination? Independent reading!

STEP INTO READING® will help your child get there. The program offers five steps to reading success. Each step includes fun stories and colorful art or photographs. In addition to original fiction and books with favorite characters, there are Step into Reading Non-Fiction Readers, Phonics Readers and Boxed Sets, Sticker Readers, and Comic Readers—a complete literacy program with something to interest every child.

Learning to Read, Step by Step!

Ready to Read   Preschool–Kindergarten
• big type and easy words • rhyme and rhythm • picture clues
For children who know the alphabet and are eager to begin reading.

Reading with Help   Preschool–Grade 1
• basic vocabulary • short sentences • simple stories
For children who recognize familiar words and sound out new words with help.

Reading on Your Own   Grades 1–3
• engaging characters • easy-to-follow plots • popular topics
For children who are ready to read on their own.

Reading Paragraphs   Grades 2–3
• challenging vocabulary • short paragraphs • exciting stories
For newly independent readers who read simple sentences with confidence.

Ready for Chapters   Grades 2–4
• chapters • longer paragraphs • full-color art
For children who want to take the plunge into chapter books but still like colorful pictures.

STEP INTO READING® is designed to give every child a successful reading experience. The grade levels are only guides; children will progress through the steps at their own speed, developing confidence in their reading.

Remember, a lifetime love of reading starts with a single step!

5

Disney·PIXAR

TALES

STEP INTO READING®

5 DISNEY·PIXAR TALES

Step 1 and 2 Books
A Collection of Five Early Readers

Random House 🏠 New York

Contents

Disney·PIXAR

FINDING NEMO

Just Keep Swimming

By Melissa Lagonegro

Illustrated By Atelier Philippe Harchy

Random House New York

Nemo has a dream.
He wants to join
the school swim team.

But Nemo has
a little fin.

He thinks that
he will never win.

Dory helps Nemo.

She teaches him
to go, go, go!

Nemo races and races.

Nemo chases and chases.

"Just keep swimming,"
Dory sings.

But Nemo thinks
of other things.

"I will never win.

I have a bad fin."

"Just keep swimming!"
Dory cries.

So Nemo tries . . .

and tries . . .

. . . and tries.

Nemo races and races.

Nemo chases and chases.

Yippee! Yahoo!

His dream comes true.

Nemo makes the team.

Can Nemo win the
first-place prize?

"Just keep swimming!"
Dory cries.

Watch him race.

Watch him chase.

Watch as Nemo wins
first place!

Disney · PIXAR

TOY STORY 3

Toy to Toy

By Tennant Redbank

Illustrated by
Caroline Egan, Adrienne Brown,
Scott Tilley, and Studio IBOIX

Random House 🏠 New York

These are Andy's toys.

Woody is a cowboy.

He wears a cowboy hat.

Buzz is a spaceman and
Woody's best friend.

Slinky is a dog.

He can stretch!

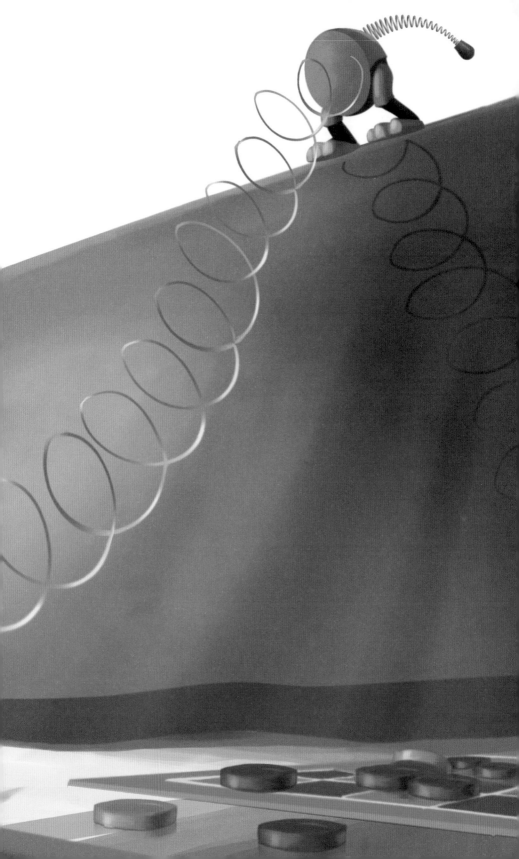

Yee-haw!
Jessie is a cowgirl.
She likes
to ride Bullseye.

Hamm is a piggy bank.

He holds pennies.

These toys are green.

They stick together.

Roar!

Rex is a dinosaur.

Andy is big now.

Andy's toys get
a new home.

They meet new toys!

Lotso is a teddy bear.

He is the boss.

Lotso likes to hug!

Big Baby is
the biggest toy.

Chunk has two faces.

Sparks spits
real sparks.

Twitch looks like
a big bad bug.

Stretch is made
of rubber.

All the toys
are ready to play!

Will Andy's toys like their new home?

Disney · PIXAR

Cars 2

SUPER SPIES

By Susan Amerikaner

Illustrated by Caroline LaVelle Egan, Scott Tilley,
Andrew Phillipson, and Seung Beom Kim

Random House 🏠 New York

Lightning McQueen is
on a plane.
He is going
to a big race.

Mater is going,

too.

He will help Lightning.

Finn and Holley
are spy cars.

Bad cars try
to hurt race cars.
Finn and Holley
must stop them.

Holley calls Mater
at the race.

Mater likes Holley.

He leaves
to meet her.

Mater sees the bad cars.

Finn fights them!

Mater is not there
to help Lightning.
Lightning loses the race!

Lightning is mad
at Mater.

Mater wants
to go home.

The bad cars follow him
to the airport.
Finn will help!

Finn and Mater race away
from the bad cars.
Finn fights the bad cars.

Mater drives
into the spy plane.
Holley waits for him.
They will escape!

Holley and Finn

tell Mater

they are spy cars.

They think Mater
is a spy car, too.
Mater will help
find the bad cars.

Holley gives Mater
spy tools.

She dresses him up
to fool the bad cars.

Now Mater

is a spy car,

too!

Mater finds
the bad cars.

They want
to hurt Lightning!

Mater tries
to warn Lightning.
But Lightning does
not see him.

The bad cars catch
Finn, Holley, and Mater.
They trap them
in a big clock.

Mater gets away!

Holley escapes,
too!
She fights the bad cars.

Mater finds Lightning.
They race away
from the bad cars.

Mater uses

his spy tools.

He and Lightning
fly up
in the air.

Mater and Lightning
go to see
the Queen.

Mater helped

Finn and Holley

stop the bad cars.

The Queen thanks him.

Mater and Lightning
are heroes!

Disney·PIXAR

BRAVE

BIG BEAR, LITTLE BEAR

By Susan Amerikaner

Illustrated by the Disney Storybook Artists

Random House 🏠 New York

Merida climbs SLOWLY.

Angus goes FAST!

The queen is QUIET.

Merida is LOUD.

Fergus and the boys PLAY.

Merida WORKS.

It is DAY.

It is NIGHT.

This man is STRONG.

This man is WEAK.

Angus is TALL.

Merida is SHORT.

Merida is NEAR.

Merida is FAR.

The Witch is OLD.

Merida is YOUNG.

The bear stands UP.
Merida falls DOWN.

The bear is DRY.

Merida is WET.

This bear is NICE.

This bear is MEAN.

This bear is BIG.

These bears are SMALL.

Fergus is

IN FRONT OF

Merida.

The bear is
BEHIND Merida.

The triplets are SAD.

The triplets are HAPPY.

Maudie is SCARED.

Merida is BRAVE!

Disney · PIXAR

MONSTERS UNIVERSITY

SCARING LESSONS

By Susan Amerikaner

Illustrated by Fabio Laguna, Lori Tyminski,
Adrienne Brown, Jeff Jenney, Frank Anduiza, and
the Disney Storybook Artists

Random House 🏠 New York

Monsters University
is a school for monsters.
In the Scaring Program,
students learn
to scare humans.

The students
must be very scary.
Mike is a student.

Sulley is a student, too.

He looks scary.

He does not study.

Mike does not look scary.

He studies.

Mike and Sulley

do not like each other.

At the final
scare test,
Mike roars at Sulley.
Sulley roars at Mike.

Sulley breaks

the dean's scream can.

She kicks them out

of the Scaring Program!

Mike and Sulley
join the Oozma Kappas.
They enter the Scare
Games as a team.

The winners will get
into the Scaring Program.
The Oozma Kappa team
wants to win!

The first event
is a race.
The teams run
into a dark tunnel.

Sulley runs ahead.

Mike runs to catch up.

Their team
is left behind.

Mike trains

the Oozma Kappas.

They work together.

One event

is a hiding game.

Don hides.

Oozma Kappa does well!

The last event
is a scaring game.
The team
must scare a robot.

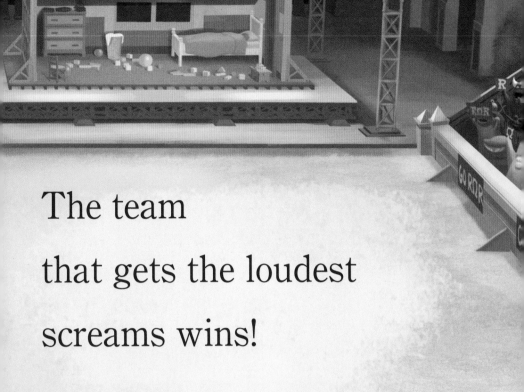

The team
that gets the loudest
screams wins!

Mike goes last.

He scares his robot.

His robot screams
the loudest!
The Oozma Kappas win!

The team cheers.
They lift Mike
up in the air.

He is a hero!

Mike checks the robot.
Sulley made
the robot scream.
Sulley cheated!
He did not think
Mike was scary enough.

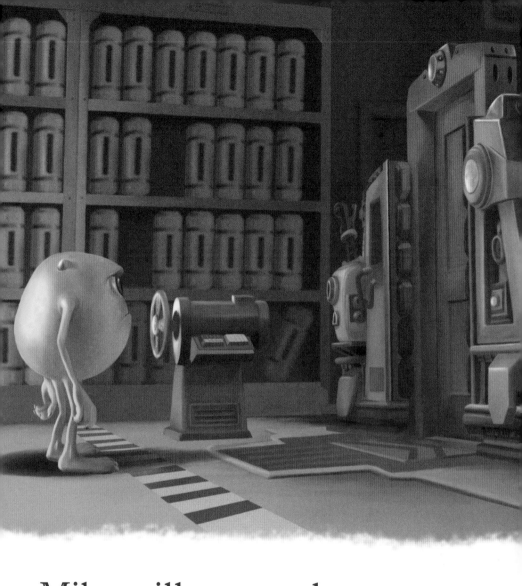

Mike will scare a human.

He wants to prove

he is scary!

Mike goes

to the human world.

He finds a cabin.

It is full of kids!

They are not scared
of Mike.
Mike is scared
of them!

Sulley finds Mike.
They need a big scream
to get home.

Sulley is scary.

Mike is smart.

They need each other!

Sulley and Mike
work together.

Mike coaches Sulley.

Sulley roars.

They scare the humans.

The humans scream.

The screams are loud!

The door opens.
Sulley and Mike
go home!

The dean is proud.
She wishes them
good luck.

Mike and Sulley
find jobs
at Monsters, Inc.!